The Spa

(The 'Sixties)

Edith Wharton

Alpha Editions

This edition published in 2024

ISBN : 9789361472336

Design and Setting By
Alpha Editions
www.alphaedis.com
Email - info@alphaedis.com

As per information held with us this book is in Public Domain.
This book is a reproduction of an important historical work. Alpha Editions uses the best technology to reproduce historical work in the same manner it was first published to preserve its original nature. Any marks or number seen are left intentionally to preserve its true form.

I

"YOU idiot!" said his wife, and threw down her cards.

I turned my head away quickly, to avoid seeing Hayley Delane's face; though why I wished to avoid it I could not have told you, much less why I should have imagined (if I did) that a man of his age and importance would notice what was happening to the wholly negligible features of a youth like myself.

I turned away so that he should not see how it hurt me to hear him called an idiot, even in joke—well, at least half in joke; yet I often thought him an idiot myself, and bad as my own poker was, I knew enough of the game to judge that his—when he wasn't attending—fully justified such an outburst from his wife. Why her sally disturbed me I couldn't have said; nor why, when it was greeted by a shrill guffaw from her "latest," young Bolton Byrne, I itched to cuff the little bounder; nor why, when Hayley Delane, on whom banter always dawned slowly but certainly, at length gave forth his low rich gurgle of appreciation—why then, most of all, I wanted to blot the whole scene from my memory. Why?

There they sat, as I had so often seen them, in Jack Alstrop's luxurious bookless library (I'm sure the rich rows behind the glass doors were hollow), while beyond the windows the pale twilight thickened to blue over Long Island lawns and woods and a moonlit streak of sea. No one ever looked out at *that*, except to conjecture what sort of weather there would be the next day for polo, or hunting, or racing, or whatever use the season required the face of nature to be put to; no one was aware of the twilight, the moon or the blue shadows—and Hayley Delane least of all. Day after day, night after night, he sat anchored at somebody's poker-table, and fumbled absently with his cards....

Yes; that was the man. He didn't even (as it was once said of a great authority on heraldry) know his own silly business; which was to hang about in his wife's train, play poker with her friends, and giggle at her nonsense and theirs. No wonder Mrs. Delane was sometimes exasperated. As she said, *she* hadn't asked him to marry her! Rather not: all their contemporaries could remember what a thunderbolt it had been on his side. The first time he had seen her—at the theater, I think: "Who's that? Over there—with the heaps of hair?"—"Oh, Leila Gracy? Why, she's not *really* pretty...." "Well, I'm going to marry her—" "Marry her? But her father's that old scoundrel Bill Gracy ... the one...." "I'm going to marry her...." "The one who's had to resign from all his clubs...." "I'm going to marry her...." And he did; and it was she, if you please, who kept him dangling, and who would and who wouldn't, until some whipper-snapper of a youth, who was meanwhile making up his mind about *her*, had finally decided in the negative.

Such had been Hayley Delane's marriage; and such, I imagined, his way of conducting most of the transactions of his futile clumsy life.... Big bursts of impulse—storms he couldn't control—then long periods of drowsing calm, during which, something made me feel, old regrets and remorses woke and stirred under the indolent surface of his nature. And yet, wasn't I simply romanticizing a commonplace case? I turned back from the window to look at the group. The bringing of candles to the card-tables had scattered pools of illumination throughout the shadowy room; in their radiance Delane's harsh head stood out like a cliff from a flowery plain. Perhaps it was only his bigness, his heaviness and swarthiness—perhaps his greater age, for he must have been at least fifteen years older than his wife and most of her friends; at any rate, I could never look at him without feeling that he belonged elsewhere, not so much in another society as in another age. For there was no doubt that the society he lived in suited him well enough. He shared cheerfully in all the amusements of his little set—rode, played polo, hunted and drove his four-in-hand with the best of them (you will see, by the last allusion, that we were still in the archaic 'nineties). Nor could I guess what other occupations he would have preferred, had he been given his choice. In spite of my admiration for him I could not bring myself to think it was Leila Gracy who had subdued him to what she worked in. What would he have chosen to do if he had not met her that night at the play? Why, I rather thought, to meet and marry somebody else just like her. No; the difference in him was not in his tastes—it was in something ever so much deeper. Yet what is deeper in a man than his tastes?

In another age, then, he would probably have been doing the equivalent of what he was doing now: idling, taking much violent exercise, eating more than was good for him, laughing at the same kind of nonsense, and worshipping, with the same kind of dull routine-worship, the same kind of woman, whether dressed in a crinoline, a farthingale, a peplum or the skins of beasts—it didn't much matter under what sumptuary dispensation one placed her. Only in that other age there might have been outlets for other faculties, now dormant, perhaps even atrophied, but which must—yes, really must—have had something to do with the building of that big friendly forehead, the monumental nose, and the rich dimple which now and then furrowed his cheek with light. Did the dimple even mean no more than Leila Gracy?

Well, perhaps it was *I* who was the idiot, if she'd only known it; an idiot to believe in her husband, be obsessed by him, oppressed by him, when, for thirty years now, he'd been only the Hayley Delane whom everybody took for granted, and was glad to see, and immediately forgot. Turning from my contemplation of that great structural head, I looked at his wife. Her head was still like something in the making, something just flowering, a girl's head ringed with haze. Even the kindly candles betrayed the lines in her face, the paint on her lips, the peroxide on her hair; but they could not lessen her fluidity of outline, or the girlishness that lurked in her eyes, floating up from their depths like a startled Naïad. There was an irreducible innocence about her, as there so often is about women who have spent their time in amassing sentimental experiences. As I looked at the husband and wife, thus confronted above the cards, I marvelled more and more that it was she who ruled and he who bent the neck. You will see by this how young I still was.

So young, indeed, that Hayley Delane had dawned on me in my school-days as an accomplished fact, a finished monument: like Trinity Church, the Reservoir or the Knickerbocker Club. A New Yorker of my generation could no more imagine him altered or away than any of those venerable institutions. And so I had continued to take him for granted till, my Harvard days over, I had come back after an interval of world-wandering to settle down in New York, and he had broken on me afresh as something still not wholly accounted for, and more interesting than I had suspected.

I don't say the matter kept me awake. I had my own business (in a down-town office), and the pleasures of my age; I was hard at work discovering New York. But now and then the Hayley Delane riddle would thrust itself between me and my other interests, as it had done tonight just because his wife had sneered at him, and he had laughed and thought her funny. And at such times I found myself moved and excited out of all proportion to anything I knew about him, or had observed in him, to justify such emotions.

The game was over, the dressing-bell had rung. It rang again presently, with a discreet insistence: Alstrop, easy in all else, preferred that his guests should not be more than half an hour late for dinner.

"I say—*Leila!*" he finally remonstrated.

The golden coils drooped above her chips. "Yes—yes. Just a minute. Hayley, you'll have to pay for me.—There, I'm going!" She laughed and pushed back her chair.

Delane, laughing also, got up lazily. Byrne flew to open the door for Mrs. Delane; the other women trooped out with her. Delane, having settled her debts, picked up her gold-mesh bag and cigarette-case, and followed.

I turned toward a window opening on the lawn. There was just time to stretch my legs while curling-tongs and powder were being plied above stairs. Alstrop joined me, and we stood staring up at a soft dishevelled sky in which the first stars came and went.

"Curse it—looks rotten for our match tomorrow!"

"Yes—but what a good smell the coming rain does give to things!"

He laughed. "You're an optimist—like old Hayley."

We strolled across the lawn toward the woodland.

"Why like old Hayley?"

"Oh, he's a regular philosopher. I've never seen him put out, have you?"

"No. That must be what makes him look so sad," I exclaimed.

"Sad? Hayley? Why, I was just saying—"

"Yes, I know. But the only people who are never put out are the people who don't care; and not caring is about the saddest occupation there is. I'd like to see him in a rage just once."

My host gave a faint whistle, and remarked: "By Jove, I believe the wind's hauling round to the north. If it does—" He moistened his finger and held it up.

I knew there was no use in theorizing with Alstrop; but I tried another tack. "What on earth has Delane done with himself all these years?" I asked. Alstrop was forty, or thereabouts, and by a good many years better able than I to cast a backward glance over the problem.

But the effort seemed beyond him. "Why—what years?"

"Well—ever since he left college."

"Lord! How do I know? I wasn't there. Hayley must be well past fifty."

It sounded formidable to my youth; almost like a geological era. And that suited him, in a way—I could imagine him drifting, or silting, or something measurable by aeons, at the rate of about a millimetre a century.

"How long has he been married?" I asked.

"I don't know that either; nearly twenty years, I should say. The kids are growing up. The boys are both at Groton. Leila doesn't look it, I must say—not in some lights."

"Well, then, what's he been doing since he married?"

"Why, what should he have done? He's always had money enough to do what he likes. He's got his partnership in the bank, of course. They say that rascally old father-in-law, whom he refuses to see, gets a good deal of money out of him. You know he's awfully soft-hearted. But he can swing it all, I fancy. Then he sits on lots of boards—Blind Asylum, Children's Aid, S.P.C.A., and all the rest. And there isn't a better sport going."

"But that's not what I mean," I persisted.

Alstrop looked at me through the darkness. "You don't mean women? I never heard—but then one wouldn't, very likely. He's a shut-up fellow."

We turned back to dress for dinner. Yes, that was the word I wanted; he was a shut-up fellow. Even the rudimentary Alstrop felt it. But shut-up consciously, deliberately—or only instinctively, congenitally? There the mystery lay.

II

THE big polo match came off the next day. It was the first of the season, and, taking respectful note of the fact, the barometer, after a night of showers, jumped back to Fair.

All Fifth Avenue had poured down to see New York versus Hempstead. The beautifully rolled lawns and freshly painted club stand were sprinkled with spring dresses and abloom with sunshades, and coaches and other vehicles without number enclosed the farther side of the field.

Hayley Delane still played polo, though he had grown so heavy that the cost of providing himself with mounts must have been considerable. He was, of course, no longer regarded as in the first rank; indeed, in these later days, when the game has become an exact science, I hardly know to what use such a weighty body as his could be put. But in that far-off dawn of the sport his sureness and swiftness of stroke caused him to be still regarded as a useful back, besides being esteemed for the part he had taken in introducing and establishing the game.

I remember little of the beginning of the game, which resembled many others I had seen. I never played myself, and I had no money on: for me the principal interest of the scene lay in the May weather, the ripple of spring dresses over the turf, the sense of youth, fun, gaiety, of young manhood and womanhood weaving their eternal pattern under the conniving sky. Now and then they were interrupted for a moment by a quick "Oh" which turned all those tangled glances the same way, as two glittering streaks of men and horses dashed across the green, locked, swayed, rayed outward into starry figures, and rolled back. But it was for a moment only—then eyes wandered again, chatter began, and youth and sex had it their own way till the next charge shook them from their trance.

I was of the number of these divided watchers. Polo as a spectacle did not amuse me for long, and I saw about as little of it as the pretty girls perched beside their swains on coach-tops and club stand. But by chance my vague wanderings brought me to the white palings enclosing the field, and there, in a cluster of spectators, I caught sight of Leila Delane.

As I approached I was surprised to notice a familiar figure shouldering away from her. One still saw old Bill Gracy often enough in the outer purlieus of the big race-courses; but I wondered how he had got into the enclosure of a fashionable Polo Club. There he was, though, unmistakably; who could forget that swelling chest under the shabby-smart racing-coat, the gray top-hat always pushed back from his thin auburn curls, and the mixture of furtiveness and swagger which made his liquid glance so pitiful? Among the figures that rose here and there like warning ruins from the dead-level of old New York's respectability, none was more typical than Bill Gracy's; my gaze followed him curiously as he shuffled away from his daughter. "Trying to get more money out of her," I concluded; and remembered what Alstrop had said of Delane's generosity.

"Well, if I were Delane," I thought, "I'd pay a good deal to keep that old ruffian out of sight."

Mrs. Delane, turning to watch her father's retreat, saw me and nodded. At the same moment Delane, on a tall deep-chested poney, ambled across the field, stick on shoulder. As he rode thus, heavily yet mightily, in his red-and-black shirt and white breeches, his head standing out like a bronze against the turf, I whimsically recalled the figure of Guidoriccio da Foligno, the famous mercenary, riding at a slow powerful pace across the fortressed fresco of the Town Hall of Siena. Why a New York banker of excessive weight and more than middle age, jogging on a poney across a Long Island polo field, should have reminded me of a martial figure on an armoured war-horse, I find it hard to explain. As far as I knew there were no turreted fortresses in Delane's background; and his too juvenile polo cap and gaudy shirt were a poor substitute for Guidoriccio's coat of mail. But it was the kind of trick the man was always playing; reminding me, in his lazy torpid way, of times and scenes and people greater than he could know. That was why he kept on interesting me.

It was this interest which caused me to pause by Mrs. Delane, whom I generally avoided. After a vague smile she had already turned her gaze on the field.

"You're admiring your husband?" I suggested, as Delane's trot carried him across our line of vision.

She glanced at me dubiously. "You think he's too fat to play, I suppose?" she retorted, a little snappishly.

"I think he's the finest figure in sight. He looks like a great general, a great soldier of fortune—in an old fresco, I mean."

She stared, perhaps suspecting irony, as she always did beneath the unintelligible.

"Ah, *he* can pay anything he likes for his mounts!" she murmured; and added, with a wandering laugh: "Do you mean it as a compliment? Shall I tell him what you say?"

"I wish you would."

But her eyes were off again, this time to the opposite end of the field. Of course—Bolton Byrne was playing on the other side! The fool of a woman was always like that—absorbed in her latest adventure. Yet there had been so many, and she must by this time have been so radiantly sure there would be more! But at every one the girl was born anew in her: she blushed, palpitated, "sat out" dances, plotted for tête-à-têtes, pressed flowers (I'll wager) in her copy of "Omar Khayyám," and was all white muslin and wild roses while it lasted. And the Byrne fever was then at its height.

It did not seem polite to leave her immediately, and I continued to watch the field at her side. "It's their last chance to score," she flung at me, leaving me to apply the ambiguous pronoun; and after that we remained silent.

The game had been a close one; the two sides were five each, and the crowd about the rails hung breathless on the last minutes. The struggle was short and swift, and dramatic enough to hold even the philanderers on the coach-tops. Once I stole a glance at Mrs. Delane, and saw the colour rush to her cheek. Byrne was hurling himself across the field, crouched on the neck of his somewhat weedy mount, his stick swung like a lance—a pretty enough sight, for he was young and supple, and light in the saddle.

"They're going to win!" she gasped with a happy cry.

But just then Byrne's poney, unequal to the pace, stumbled, faltered, and came down. His rider dropped from the saddle, hauled the animal to his feet, and stood for a minute half-dazed before he scrambled up again. That minute made the difference. It gave the other side their chance. The knot of men and horses tightened, wavered, grew loose, broke up in arrowing flights; and suddenly a ball—Delane's—sped through the enemy's goal, victorious. A roar of delight went up; "Good for old Hayley!" voices shouted. Mrs. Delane gave a little sour laugh. "That—that beastly poney; I warned him it was no good—and the ground still so slippery," she broke out.

"The poney? Why, he's a ripper. It's not every mount that will carry Delane's weight," I said. She stared at me unseeingly and turned away with twitching lips. I saw her speeding off toward the enclosure.

I followed hastily, wanting to see Delane in the moment of his triumph. I knew he took all these little sporting successes with an absurd seriousness, as if, mysteriously, they were the shadow of more substantial achievements, dreamed of, or accomplished, in some previous life. And perhaps the elderly man's vanity in holding his own with the youngsters was also an element of his satisfaction; how could one tell, in a mind of such monumental simplicity?

When I reached the saddling enclosure I did not at once discover him; an unpleasant sight met my eyes instead. Bolton Byrne, livid and withered—his face like an old woman's, I thought—rode across the empty field, angrily lashing his poney's flanks. He slipped to the ground, and as he did so, struck the shivering animal a last blow clean across the head. An unpleasant sight—

But retribution fell. It came like a black-and-red thunderbolt descending on the wretch out of the heaven. Delane had him by the collar, had struck him with his whip across the shoulders, and then flung him off like a thing too mean for human handling. It was over in the taking of a breath—then, while the crowd hummed and closed in, leaving Byrne to slink away as if he had become invisible, I saw my big Delane, grown calm and apathetic, turn to the poney and lay a soothing hand on its neck.

I was pushing forward, moved by the impulse to press that hand, when his wife went up to him. Though I was not far off I could not hear what she said; people did not speak loud in those days, or "make scenes," and the two or three words which issued from Mrs. Delane's lips must have been inaudible to everyone but her husband. On his dark face they raised a sudden redness; he made a motion of his free arm (the other hand still on the poney's neck), as if to wave aside an importunate child; then he felt in his pocket, drew out a cigarette, and lit it. Mrs. Delane, white as a ghost, was hurrying back to Alstrop's coach.

I was turning away too when I saw her husband hailed again. This time it was Bill Gracy, shoving and yet effacing himself, as his manner was, who came up, a facile tear on his lashes, his smile half tremulous, half defiant, a yellow-gloved hand held out.

"God bless you for it, Hayley—God bless you, my dear boy!"

Delane's hand reluctantly left the poney's neck. It wavered for an instant, just touched the other's palm, and was instantly engulfed in it. Then Delane, without speaking, turned toward the shed where his mounts were being rubbed down, while his father-in-law swaggered from the scene.

I had promised, on the way home, to stop for tea at a friend's house half-way between the Polo Club and Alstrop's. Another friend, who was also going there, offered me a lift, and carried me on to Alstrop's afterward.

During our drive, and about the tea-table, the talk of course dwelt mainly on the awkward incident of Bolton Byrne's thrashing. The women were horrified or admiring, as their humour moved them; but the men all agreed that it was natural enough. In such a case any pretext was permissible, they said; though it was stupid of Hayley to air his grievance on a public occasion. But then he *was* stupid—that was the consensus of opinion. If there was a blundering way of doing a thing that needed to be done, trust him to hit on it! For the rest, everyone spoke of him affectionately, and agreed that Leila was a fool ... and nobody particularly liked Byrne, an "outsider" who had pushed himself into society by means of cheek and showy horsemanship. But Leila, it was agreed, had always had a weakness for "outsiders," perhaps because their admiration flattered her extreme desire to be thought "in."

"Wonder how many of the party you'll find left—this affair must have caused a good deal of a shake-up," my friend said, as I got down at Alstrop's door; and the same thought was in my own mind. Byrne would be gone, of course; and no doubt, in another direction, Delane and Leila. I wished I had a chance to shake that blundering hand of Hayley's....

Hall and drawing-room were empty; the dressing-bell must have sounded its discreet appeal more than once, and I was relieved to find it had been heeded. I didn't want to stumble on any of my fellow-guests till I had seen our host. As I was dashing upstairs I heard him call me from the library, and turned back.

"No hurry—dinner put off till nine," he said cheerfully; and added, on a note of inexpressible relief: "We've had a tough job of it—*ouf!*"

The room looked as if they had: the card tables stood untouched, and the deep armchairs, gathered into confidential groups, seemed still deliberating on the knotty problem. I noticed that a good deal of whiskey and soda had gone toward its solution.

"What happened? Has Byrne left?"

"Byrne? No—thank goodness!" Alstrop looked at me almost reproachfully. "Why should he? That was just what we wanted to avoid."

"I don't understand. You don't mean that *he's* stayed and the Delanes have gone?"

"Lord forbid! Why should they, either? Hayley's apologized!"

My jaw fell, and I returned my host's stare.

"Apologized? To that hound? For what?"

Alstrop gave an impatient shrug. "Oh, for God's sake don't reopen the cursèd question," it seemed to say. Aloud he echoed: "For what? Why, after all, a man's got a right to thrash his own poney, hasn't he? It was beastly unsportsmanlike, of course—but it's nobody's business if Byrne chooses to be that kind of a cad. That's what Hayley saw—when he cooled down."

"Then I'm sorry he cooled down."

Alstrop looked distinctly annoyed. "I don't follow you. We had a hard enough job. You said you wanted to see him in a rage just once; but you don't want him to go on making an ass of himself, do you?"

"I don't call it making an ass of himself to thrash Byrne."

"And to advertise his conjugal difficulties all over Long Island, with twenty newspaper reporters at his heels?"

I stood silent, baffled but incredulous. "I don't believe he ever gave that a thought. I wonder who put it to him first in that way?"

Alstrop twisted his unlit cigarette about in his fingers. "We all did—as delicately as we could. But it was Leila who finally convinced him. I must say Leila was very game."

I still pondered: the scene in the paddock rose again before me, the quivering agonized animal, and the way Delane's big hand had been laid reassuringly on its neck.

"Nonsense! I don't believe a word of it!" I declared.

"A word of what I've been telling you?"

"Well, of the official version of the case."

To my surprise, Alstrop met my glance with an eye neither puzzled nor resentful. A shadow seemed to be lifted from his honest face.

"What *do* you believe?" he asked.

"Why, that Delane thrashed that cur for ill-treating the poney, and not in the least for being too attentive to Mrs. Delane. I was there, I tell you—I saw him."

Alstrop's brow cleared completely. "There's something to be said for that theory," he agreed, smiling over the match he was holding to his cigarette.

"Well, then—what was there to apologize for?"

"Why, for *that*—butting in between Byrne and his horse. Don't you see, you young idiot? If Hayley hadn't apologized, the mud was bound to stick to his wife. Everybody would have said the row was on her account.

It's as plain as the knob on the door—there wasn't anything else for him to do. He saw it well enough after she'd said a dozen words to him—"

"I wonder what those words were," I muttered.

"Don't know. He and she came downstairs together. He looked a hundred years old, poor old chap. 'It's the cruelty, it's the cruelty,' he kept saying; 'I hate cruelty.' I rather think he knows we're all on his side. Anyhow, it's all patched up and well patched up; and I've ordered my last 'eighty-four Georges Goulet brought up for dinner. Meant to keep it for my own wedding-breakfast; but since this afternoon I've rather lost interest in that festivity," Alstrop concluded with a celibate grin.

"Well," I repeated, as though it were a relief to say, "I could swear he did it for the poney."

"Oh, so could I," my host acquiesced as we went upstairs together.

On my threshold, he took me by the arm and followed me in. I saw there was still something on his mind.

"Look here, old chap—you say you were in there when it happened?"

"Yes. Close by—"

"Well," he interrupted, "for the Lord's sake don't allude to the subject tonight, will you?"

"Of course not."

"Thanks a lot. Truth is, it was a narrow squeak, and I couldn't help admiring the way Leila played up. She was in a fury with Hayley; but she got herself in hand in no time, and behaved very decently. She told me privately he was often like that—flaring out all of a sudden like a madman. You wouldn't imagine it, would you, with that quiet way of his? She says she thinks it's his old wound."

"What old wound?"

"Didn't you know he was wounded—where was it? Bull Run, I believe. In the head—"

No, I hadn't known; hadn't even heard, or remembered, that Delane had been in the Civil War. I stood and stared in my astonishment.

"Hayley Delane? In the war?"

"Why, of course. All through it."

"But Bull Run—Bull Run was at the very beginning." I broke off to go through a rapid mental calculation. "Look here, Jack, it can't be; he's not over fifty-five. You told me so yourself. If he was in it from the beginning he must have gone into it as a schoolboy."

"Well, that's just what he did: ran away from school to volunteer. His family didn't know what had become of him till he was wounded. I remember hearing my people talk about it. Great old sport, Hayley. I'd have given a lot not to have this thing happen; not at my place anyhow; but it *has*, and there's no help for it. Look here, you swear you won't make a sign, will you? I've got all the others into line, and if you'll back us up we'll have a regular Happy Family Evening. Jump into your clothes—it's nearly nine."

III

THIS is not a story-teller's story; it is not even the kind of episode capable of being shaped into one. Had it been, I should have reached my climax, or at any rate its first stage, in the incident at the Polo Club, and what I have left to tell would be the effect of that incident on the lives of the three persons concerned.

It is not a story, or anything in the semblance of a story, but merely an attempt to depict for you—and in so doing, perhaps make clearer to myself—the aspect and character of a man whom I loved, perplexedly but faithfully, for many years. I make no apology, therefore, for the fact that Bolton Byrne, whose evil shadow ought to fall across all my remaining pages, never again appears in them; and that the last I saw of him (for my purpose) was when, after our exaggeratedly cheerful and even noisy dinner that evening at Jack Alstrop's, I observed him shaking hands with Hayley Delane, and declaring, with pinched lips and a tone of falsetto cordiality: "Bear malice? Well, rather not—why, what rot! All's fair in—in polo, ain't it? I should say so! Yes—off first thing tomorrow. S'pose of course you're staying on with Jack over Sunday? I wish I hadn't promised the Gildermeres—." And therewith he vanishes, having served his purpose as a passing lantern-flash across the twilight of Hayley Delane's character.

All the while, I continued to feel that it was not Bolton Byrne who mattered. While clubs and drawing-rooms twittered with the episode, and friends grew portentous in trying to look unconscious, and said "I don't know what you mean," with eyes beseeching you to speak if you knew more than they did, I had already discarded the whole affair, as I was sure Delane had. "It *was* the poney, and nothing but the poney," I chuckled to myself, as pleased as if I had owed Mrs. Delane a grudge, and were exulting in her abasement; and still there ran through my mind the phrase which Alstrop said Delane had kept repeating: "It was the cruelty—it was the cruelty. I hate cruelty."

How it fitted in, now, with the other fact my host had let drop—the fact that Delane had fought all through the civil war! It seemed incredible that it should have come to me as a surprise; that I should have forgotten, or perhaps never even known, this phase of his history. Yet in young men like myself, just out of college in the 'nineties, such ignorance was more excusable than now seems possible.

That was the dark time of our national indifference, before the country's awakening; no doubt the war seemed much farther from us, much less a part of us, than it does to the young men of today. Such was the case, at any rate, in old New York, and more particularly, perhaps, in the little clan of well-to-do and indolent old New Yorkers among whom I had grown up. Some of these, indeed, had fought bravely through the four years: New York had borne her part, a memorable part, in the long struggle. But I remember with what perplexity I first wakened to the fact—it was in my school-days—that if certain of my father's kinsmen and contemporaries had been in the war, others—how many!—had stood aside. I recall especially the shock with which, at school, I had heard a boy explain his father's lameness: "He's never got over that shot in the leg he got at Chancellorsville."

I stared; for my friend's father was just my own father's age. At the moment (it was at a school foot-ball match) the two men were standing side by side, in full sight of us—*his* father stooping, halt and old, mine, even to filial eyes, straight and youthful. Only an hour before I had been bragging to my friend about the wonderful shot my father was (he had taken me down to his North Carolina shooting at Christmas); but now I stood abashed.

The next time I went home for the holidays I said to my mother, one day when we were alone: "Mother, why didn't father fight in the war?" My heart was beating so hard that I thought she must have seen my excitement and been shocked. But she raised an untroubled face from her embroidery.

"Your father, dear? Why, because he was a married man." She had a reminiscent smile. "Molly was born already—she was six months old when Fort Sumter fell. I remember I was nursing her when Papa came in with the news. We couldn't believe it." She paused to match a silk placidly. "Married men weren't called upon to fight," she explained.

"But they *did*, though, Mother! Payson Gray's father fought. He was so badly wounded at Chancellorsville that he's had to walk with a stick ever since."

"Well, my dear, I don't suppose you would want your Papa to be like that, would you?" She paused again, and finding I made no answer, probably thought it pained me to be thus convicted of heartlessness, for she added, as if softening the rebuke: "Two of your father's cousins *did* fight: his cousins Harold and James. They were young men, with no family obligations. And poor Jamie was killed, you remember."

I listened in silence, and never again spoke to my mother of the war. Nor indeed to anyone—even myself. I buried the whole business out of sight, out of hearing, as I thought. After all, the war had all happened long ago; it had been over ten years when I was born. And nobody ever talked about it nowadays. Still, one did, of course, as one grew up, meet older men of whom it was said: "Yes, so-and-so was in the war." Many of them even continued to be known by the military titles with which they had left the service: Colonel Ruscott, Major Detrancy, old General Scole. People smiled a little, but admitted that, if it pleased them to keep their army rank, it was a right they had earned. Hayley Delane, it appeared, thought differently. He had never allowed himself to be called "Major" or "Colonel" (I think he had left the service a Colonel). And besides he was years younger than these veterans. To find that he had fought at their side was like discovering that the grandmother one could remember playing with had been lifted up by her nurse to see General Washington. I always thought of Hayley Delane as belonging to my own generation rather than to my father's; though I knew him to be so much older than myself, and occasionally called him "sir," I felt on an equality with him, the equality produced by sharing the same amusements and talking of them in the same slang. And indeed he must have been ten or fifteen years younger than the few men I knew who had been in the war, none of whom, I was sure, had had to run away from school to volunteer; so that my forgetfulness (or perhaps even ignorance) of his past was not inexcusable.

Broad and Delane had been, for two or three generations, one of the safe and conservative private banks of New York. My friend Hayley had been made a partner early in his career; the post was almost hereditary in his family. It happened that, not long after the scene at Alstrop's, I was offered a position in the house. The offer came, not through Delane, but through Mr. Frederick Broad, the senior member, who was an old friend of my father's. The chance was too advantageous to be rejected, and I transferred to a desk at Broad and Delane's my middling capacities and my earnest desire to do my best. It was owing to this accidental change that there gradually grew up between Hayley Delane and myself a sentiment almost filial on my part, elder-brotherly on his—for paternal one could hardly call him, even with his children.

My job need not have thrown me in his way, for his business duties sat lightly on him, and his hours at the bank were neither long nor regular. But he appeared to take a liking to me, and soon began to call on me for the many small services which, in the world of affairs, a young man can render his elders. His great perplexity was the writing of business letters. He knew what he wanted to say; his sense of the proper use of words was clear and prompt; I never knew anyone more impatient of the hazy verbiage with which American primary culture was already corrupting our speech. He would put his finger at once on these laborious inaccuracies, growling: "For God's sake, translate it into English—" but when he had to write, or worse still dictate, a letter his friendly forehead and big hands grew damp, and he would mutter, half to himself and half to me: "How the devil shall I say: 'Your letter of the blankth came yesterday, and after thinking over what you propose I don't like the looks of it'?"—"Why, say just that," I would answer; but he would shake his head and object: "My dear fellow, you're as bad as I am. You don't know how *to write good English*." In his mind there was a gulf fixed between speaking and writing the language. I could never get his imagination to bridge this gulf, or to see that the phrases which fell from his lips were "better English" than the written version, produced after much toil and pen-biting, which consisted in translating the same statement into some such language as: "I am in receipt of your communication of the 30th ultimo, and regret to be compelled to inform you in reply that, after mature consideration of the proposals therein contained, I find myself unable to pronounce a favourable judgment upon the same"—usually sending a furious dash through "the same" as "counterjumper's lingo," and then groaning over his inability to find a more Johnsonian substitute.

"The trouble with me," he used to say, "is that both my parents were martinets on grammar, and never let any of us children use a vulgar expression without correcting us." (By "vulgar" he meant either familiar or inexact.) "We were brought up on the best books—Scott and Washington Irving, old what's-his-name who wrote the *Spectator*, and Gibbon and so forth; and though I'm not a literary man, and never set up to be, I can't forget my early training, and when I see the children reading a newspaper-fellow like Kipling I want to tear the rubbish out of their hands. Cheap journalism—that's what most modern books are. And you'll excuse my saying, dear boy, that even you are too young to know how English ought to be *written*."

It was quite true—though I had at first found it difficult to believe—that Delane must once have been a reader. He surprised me, one night, as we were walking home from a dinner where we had met, by apostrophizing the moon, as she rose, astonished, behind the steeple of the "Heavenly Rest," with "She walks in beauty like the night"; and he was fond of describing a victorious charge in a polo match by saying: "Tell you what, we came down on 'em like the Assyrian." Nor had Byron been his only fare. There had evidently been a time when he had known the whole of "Gray's Elegy" by heart, and I once heard him murmuring to himself, as we stood together one autumn evening on the terrace of his country-house:

Now fades the glimmering landscape on the sight,
And all the air a solemn stillness holds....

Little sympathy as I felt for Mrs. Delane, I could not believe it was his marriage which had checked Delane's interest in books. To judge from his very limited stock of allusions and quotations, his reading seemed to have ceased a good deal earlier than his first meeting with Leila Gracy. Exploring him like a geologist, I found, for several layers under the Leila stratum, no trace of any interest in letters; and I concluded that, like other men I knew, his mind had been receptive up to a certain age, and had then snapped shut on what it possessed, like a replete crustacean never reached by another high tide. People, I had by this time found, all stopped living at one time or another, however many years longer they continued to be alive; and I suspected that Delane had stopped at about nineteen. That date would roughly coincide with the end of the civil war, and with his return to the common-place existence from which he had never since deviated. Those four years had apparently filled to the brim every crevice of his being. For I could not hold that he had gone through them unawares, as some famous figures, puppets of fate, have been tossed from heights to depths of human experience without once knowing what was happening to them—forfeiting a crown by the insistence on some prescribed ceremonial, or by carrying on their flight a certain monumental dressing-case.

No, Hayley Delane had felt the war, had been made different by it; how different I saw only when I compared him to the other "veterans" who, from being regarded by me as the dullest of my father's dinner-guests, were now become figures of absorbing interest. Time was when, at my mother's announcement that General Scole or Major Detrancy was coming to dine, I had invariably found a pretext for absenting myself; now, when I knew they were expected, my chief object was to persuade her to invite Delane.

"But he's so much younger—he cares only for the sporting set. He won't be flattered at being asked with old gentlemen." And my mother, with a slight smile, would add: "If Hayley has a weakness, it's the wish to be thought younger than he is—on his wife's account, I suppose."

Once, however, she did invite him, and he accepted; and we got over having to ask Mrs. Delane (who undoubtedly *would* have been bored) by leaving out Mrs. Scole and Mrs. Ruscott, and making it a "man's dinner" of the old-fashioned sort, with canvas-backs, a bowl of punch, and my mother the only lady present—the kind of evening my father still liked best.

I remember, at that dinner, how attentively I studied the contrasts, and tried to detect the points of resemblance, between General Scole, old Detrancy and Delane. Allusions to the war—anecdotes of Bull Run and Andersonville, of Lincoln, Seward and MacClellan, were often on Major Detrancy's lips, especially after the punch had gone round. "When a fellow's been through the war," he used to say as a preface to almost everything, from expressing his opinion of last Sunday's sermon to praising the roasting of a canvas-back. Not so General Scole. No one knew exactly why he had been raised to the rank he bore, but he tacitly proclaimed his right to it by never alluding to the subject. He was a tall and silent old gentleman with a handsome shock of white hair, half-shut blue eyes glinting between veined lids, and an impressively upright carriage. His manners were perfect—so perfect that they stood him in lieu of language, and people would say afterward how agreeable he had been when he had only bowed and smiled, and got up and sat down again, with an absolute mastery of those difficult arts. He was said to be a judge of horses and Madeira, but he never rode, and was reported to give very indifferent wines to the rare guests he received in his grim old house in Irving Place.

He and Major Detrancy had one trait in common—the extreme caution of the old New Yorker. They viewed with instinctive distrust anything likely to derange their habits, diminish their comfort, or lay on them any unwonted responsibilities, civic or social; and slow as their other mental processes were, they showed a supernatural quickness in divining when a seemingly harmless conversation might draw them into "signing a paper," backing up even the mildest attempt at municipal reform, or pledging them to support, on however small a scale, any new and unfamiliar cause.

According to their creed, gentlemen subscribed as handsomely as their means allowed to the Charity Organization Society, the Patriarchs Balls, the Children's Aid, and their own parochial charities. Everything beyond savoured of "politics," revivalist meetings, or the attempts of vulgar persons to buy their way into the circle of the elect; even the Society for the Prevention of Cruelty to Animals, being of more recent creation, seemed open to doubt, and they thought it rash of certain members of the clergy to lend it their names. "But then," as Major Detrancy said, "in this noisy age some people will do anything to attract notice." And they breathed a joint sigh over the vanished "Old New York" of their youth, the exclusive and impenetrable New York to which Rubini and Jenny Lind had sung and Mr. Thackeray lectured, the New York which had declined to receive Charles Dickens, and which, out of revenge, he had so scandalously ridiculed.

Yet Major Detrancy and General Scole had fought all through the war, had participated in horrors and agonies untold, endured all manner of hardships and privations, suffered the extremes of heat and cold, hunger, sickness and wounds; and it had all faded like an indigestion comfortably slept off, leaving them perfectly commonplace and happy.

The same was true, with a difference, of Colonel Ruscott, who, though not by birth of the same group, had long since been received into it, partly because he was a companion in arms, partly because of having married a Hayley connection. I can see Colonel Ruscott still: a dapper handsome little fellow, rather too much of both, with a lustrous wave to his hair (or was it a wig?), and a dash too much of Cologne on too-fine cambric. He had been in the New York militia in his youth, had "gone out" with the great Seventh; and the Seventh, ever since, had been the source and centre of his being, as still, to some octogenarians, their University dinner is.

Colonel Ruscott specialized in chivalry. For him the war was "the blue and the grey," the rescue of lovely Southern girls, anecdotes about Old Glory, and the carrying of vital despatches through the enemy lines. Enchantments seemed to have abounded in his path during the four years which had been so drab and desolate to many; and the punch (to the amusement of us youngsters, who were not above drawing him) always evoked from his memory countless situations in which by prompt, respectful yet insinuating action, he had stamped his image indelibly on some proud Southern heart, while at the same time discovering where Jackson's guerillas lay, or at what point the river was fordable.

And there sat Hayley Delane, so much younger than the others, yet seeming at such times so much their elder that I thought to myself: "But if *he* stopped growing up at nineteen, they're still in long-clothes!" But it was only morally that he had gone on growing. Intellectually they were all on a par. When the last new play at Wallack's was discussed, or my mother tentatively alluded to the last new novel by the author of *Robert Elsmere* (it was her theory that, as long as the hostess was present at a man's dinner, she should keep the talk at the highest level), Delane's remarks were no more penetrating than his neighbours'—and he was almost sure not to have read the novel.

It was when any social question was raised: any of the problems concerning club administration, charity, or the relation between "gentlemen" and the community, that he suddenly stood out from them, not so much opposed as aloof.

He would sit listening, stroking my sister's long skye-terrier (who, defying all rules, had jumped up to his knees at dessert), with a grave half-absent look on his heavy face; and just as my mother (I knew) was thinking how bored he was, that big smile of his would reach out and light up his dimple, and he would say, with enough diffidence to mark his respect for his elders, yet a complete independence of their views: "After all, what does it matter who makes the first move? The thing is to get the business done."

That was always the gist of it. To everyone else, my father included, what mattered in everything, from Diocesan Meetings to Patriarchs Balls, was just what Delane seemed so heedless of: the standing of the people who made up the committee or headed the movement. To Delane, only the movement itself counted; if the thing was worth doing, he pronounced in his slow lazy way, get it done somehow, even if its backers *were* Methodists or Congregationalists, or people who dined in the middle of the day.

"If they were convicts from Sing Sing I shouldn't care," he affirmed, his hand lazily flattering the dog's neck as I had seen it caress Byrne's terrified poney.

"Or lunatics out of Bloomingdale—as these 'reformers' usually are," my father added, softening the remark with his indulgent smile.

"Oh, well," Delane murmured, his attention flagging, "I daresay we're well enough off as we are."

"Especially," added Major Detrancy with a playful sniff, "with the punch in the offing, as I perceive it to be."

The punch struck the note for my mother's withdrawal. She rose with her shy circular smile, while the gentlemen, all on their feet, protested gallantly at her desertion.

"Abandoning us to go back to Mr. Elsmere—we shall be jealous of the gentleman!" Colonel Ruscott declared, chivalrously reaching the door first; and as he opened it my father said, again with his indulgent smile: "Ah, my wife—she's a great reader."

Then the punch was brought.

IV

"YOU'LL admit," Mrs. Delane challenged me, "that Hayley's perfect."

Don't imagine you have yet done with Mrs. Delane, any more than Delane had, or I. Hitherto I have shown you only one side, or rather one phase, of her; that during which, for obvious reasons, Hayley became an obstacle or a burden. In the intervals between her great passions, when somebody had to occupy the vacant throne in her bosom, her husband was always reinstated there; and during these inter-lunar periods he and the children were her staple subjects of conversation. If you had met her then for the first time you would have taken her for the perfect wife and mother, and wondered if Hayley ever got a day off; and you would not have been far wrong in conjecturing that he seldom did.

Only these intervals were rather widely spaced, and usually of short duration; and at other times, his wife being elsewhere engaged, it was Delane who elder-brothered his big boys and their little sister. Sometimes, on these occasions—when Mrs. Delane was abroad or at Newport—Delane used to carry me off for a week to the quiet old house in the New Jersey hills, full of Hayley and Delane portraits, of heavy mahogany furniture and the mingled smell of lavender bags and leather—leather boots, leather gloves, leather luggage, all the aromas that emanate from the cupboards and passages of a house inhabited by hard riders.

When his wife was at home he never seemed to notice the family portraits or the old furniture. Leila carried off her own regrettable origin by professing a democratic scorn of ancestors in general. "I know enough bores in the flesh without bothering to remember all the dead ones," she said one day, when I had asked her the name of a stern-visaged old forbear in breast-plate and buff jerkin who hung on the library wall: and Delane, so practised in sentimental duplicities, winked jovially at the children, as who should say: "There's the proper American spirit for you, my dears! That's the way we all ought to feel."

Perhaps, however, he detected a tinge of irritation in my own look, for that evening, as we sat over the fire after Leila had yawned herself off to bed, he glanced up at the armoured image, and said: "That's old Durward Hayley—the friend of Sir Harry Vane the Younger and all that lot. I have some curious letters somewhere.... But Leila's right, you know," he added loyally.

"In not being interested?"

"In regarding all that old past as dead. It *is* dead. We've got no use for it over here. That's what that queer fellow in Washington always used to say to me...."

"What queer fellow in Washington?"

"Oh, a sort of big backwoodsman who was awfully good to me when I was in hospital ... after Bull Run...."

I sat up abruptly. It was the first time that Delane had mentioned his life during the war. I thought my hand was on the clue; but it wasn't.

"You were in hospital in Washington?"

"Yes; for a longish time. They didn't know much about disinfecting wounds in those days.... But Leila," he resumed, with his smiling obstinacy, "Leila's dead right, you know. It's a better world now. Think of what has been done to relieve suffering since then!" When he pronounced the word "suffering" the vertical furrows in his forehead deepened as though he felt the actual pang of his old wound. "Oh, I believe in progress every bit as much as *she* does—I believe we're working out toward something better. If we weren't...." He shrugged his mighty shoulders, reached lazily for the adjoining tray, and mixed my glass of whiskey-and-soda.

"But the war—you were wounded at Bull Run?"

"Yes." He looked at his watch. "But I'm off to bed now. I promised the children to take them for an early canter tomorrow, before lessons, and I have to have my seven or eight hours of sleep to feel fit. I'm getting on, you see. Put out the lights when you come up."

No; he wouldn't talk about the war.

It was not long afterward that Mrs. Delane appealed to me to testify to Hayley's perfection. She had come back from her last absence—a six weeks' flutter at Newport—rather painfully subdued and pinched-looking. For the first time I saw in the corners of her mouth that middle-aged droop which has nothing to do with the loss of teeth. "How common-looking she'll be in a few years!" I thought uncharitably.

"Perfect—perfect," she insisted; and then, plaintively: "And yet—"

I echoed coldly: "And yet?"

"With the children, for instance. He's everything to them. He's cut me out with my own children." She was half joking, half whimpering.

Presently she stole an eye-lashed look at me, and added: "And at times he's so *hard*."

"Delane?"

"Oh, I know you won't believe it. But in business matters—have you never noticed? You wouldn't admit it, I suppose. But there are times when one simply can't move him." We were in the library, and she glanced up at the breast-plated forbear. "He's as hard to the touch as *that*." She pointed to the steel convexity.

"Not the Delane I know," I murmured, embarrassed by these confidences.

"Ah, you think you know him?" she half-sneered; then, with a dutiful accent: "I've always said he was a perfect father—and he's made the children think so. And yet—"

He came in, and dropping a pale smile on him she drifted away, calling to her children.

I thought to myself: "She's getting on, and something has told her so at Newport. Poor thing!"

Delane looked as preoccupied as she did; but he said nothing till after she had left us that evening. Then he suddenly turned to me.

"Look here. You're a good friend of ours. Will you help me to think out a rather bothersome question?"

"Me, sir?" I said, surprised by the "ours," and overcome by so solemn an appeal from my elder.

He made a wan grimace. "Oh, don't call me 'sir'; not during this talk." He paused, and then added: "You're remembering the difference in our ages. Well, that's just why I'm asking you. I want the opinion of somebody who hasn't had time to freeze into his rut—as most of my contemporaries have. The fact is, I'm trying to make my wife see that we've got to let her father come and live with us."

My open-mouthed amazement must have been marked enough to pierce his gloom, for he gave a slight laugh. "Well, yes—"

I sat dumbfounded. All New York knew what Delane thought of his suave father-in-law. He had married Leila in spite of her antecedents; but Bill Gracy, at the outset, had been given to understand that he would not be received under the Delane roof. Mollified by the regular payment of a handsome allowance, the old gentleman, with tears in his eyes, was wont to tell his familiars that personally he didn't blame his son-in-law. "Our tastes differ: that's all. Hayley's not a bad chap at heart; give you my word he isn't." And the familiars, touched by such magnanimity, would pledge Hayley in the champagne provided by his last remittance.

Delane, as I still remained silent, began to explain. "You see, somebody's got to look after him—who else is there?"

"But—" I stammered.

"You'll say he's always needed looking after? Well, I've done my best; short of having him here. For a long time that seemed impossible; I quite agreed with Leila—" (So it was Leila who had banished her father!) "But now," Delane continued, "it's different. The poor old chap's getting on: he's been breaking up very fast this last year. And some bloodsucker of a woman has got hold of him, and threatened to rake up old race-course rows, and I don't know what. If we don't take him in he's bound to go under. It's his last chance—he feels it is. He's scared; he wants to come."

I was still silent, and Delane went on: "You think, I suppose, what's the use? Why not let him stew in his own juice? With a decent allowance, of course. Well, I can't say ... I can't tell you ... only I feel it mustn't be...."

"And Mrs. Delane?"

"Oh, I see her point. The children are growing up; they've hardly known their grandfather. And having him in the house isn't going to be like having a nice old lady in a cap knitting by the fire. He takes up room, Gracy does; it's not going to be pleasant. She thinks we ought to consider the children first. But I don't agree. The world's too ugly a place; why should anyone grow up thinking it's a flower-garden? Let 'em take their chance.... And then"—he hesitated, as if embarrassed—"well, you know her; she's fond of society. Why shouldn't she be? She's made for it. And of course it'll cut us off, prevent our inviting people. She won't like that, though she doesn't admit that it has anything to do with her objecting."

So, after all, he judged the wife he still worshipped! I was beginning to see why he had that great structural head, those large quiet movements. There *was* something—

"What alternative does Mrs. Delane propose?"

He coloured. "Oh, more money. I sometimes fancy," he brought out, hardly above a whisper, "that she thinks I've suggested having him here because I don't want to give more money. She won't understand, you see, that more money would just precipitate things."

I coloured too, ashamed of my own thought. Had she not, perhaps, understood; was it not her perspicacity which made her hold out? If her father was doomed to go under, why prolong the process? I could not be sure, now, that Delane did not suspect this also, and allow for it. There was apparently no limit to what he allowed for.

"*You'll* never be frozen into a rut," I ventured, smiling.

"Perhaps not frozen; but sunk down deep. I'm that already. Give me a hand up, do!" He answered my smile.

I was still in the season of cocksureness, and at a distance could no doubt have dealt glibly with the problem. But at such short range, and under those melancholy eyes, I had a chastening sense of inexperience.

"You don't care to tell me what you think?" He spoke almost reproachfully.

"Oh, it's not that.... I'm trying to. But it's so—so awfully evangelical," I brought out—for some of us were already beginning to read the Russians.

"Is it? Funny, that, too. For I have an idea I got it, with other things, from an old heathen; that chap I told you about, who used to come and talk to me by the hour in Washington."

My interest revived. "That chap in Washington—was he a heathen?"

"Well, he didn't go to church." Delane did, regularly taking the children, while Leila slept off the previous night's poker, and joining in the hymns in a robust barytone, always half a tone flat.

He seemed to guess that I found his reply inadequate, and added helplessly: "You know I'm no scholar: I don't know what you'd call him." He lowered his voice to add: "I don't think he believed in our Lord. Yet he taught me Christian charity."

"He must have been an unusual sort of man, to have made such an impression on you. What was his name?"

"There's the pity! I must have heard it, but I was all foggy with fever most of the time, and can't remember. Nor what became of him either. One day he didn't turn up—that's all I recall. And soon afterward I was off again, and didn't think of him for years. Then, one day, I had to settle something with myself, and, by George, there he was, telling me the right and wrong of it! Queer—he comes like that, at long intervals; turning-points, I suppose." He frowned, his heavy head sunk forward, his eyes distant, pursuing the vision.

"Well—hasn't he come this time?"

"Rather! That's my trouble—I can't see things in any way but his. And I want another eye to help me."

My heart was beating rather excitedly. I felt small, trivial and inadequate, like an intruder on some grave exchange of confidences.

I tried to postpone my reply, and at the same time to satisfy another curiosity. "Have you ever told Mrs. Delane about—about him?"

Delane roused himself and turned to look at me. He lifted his shaggy eyebrows slightly, protruded his lower lip, and sank once more into abstraction.

"Well, sir," I said, answering the look, "*I* believe in him."

The blood rose in his dark cheek. He turned to me again, and for a second the dimple twinkled through his gloom. "That's your answer?"

I nodded breathlessly.

He got up, walked the length of the room, and came back, pausing in front of me. "He just vanished. I never even knew his name...."

V

DELANE was right; having Bill Gracy under one's roof was not like harbouring a nice old lady. I looked on at the sequence of our talk and marvelled.

New York—the Delanes' New York—sided unhesitatingly with Leila. Society's attitude toward drink and dishonesty was still inflexible: a man who had had to resign from his clubs went down into a pit presumably bottomless. The two or three people who thought Delane's action "rather fine" made haste to add: "But he ought to have taken a house for the old man in some quiet place in the country." Bill Gracy cabined in a quiet place in the country! Within a week he would have set the neighbourhood on fire. He was simply not to be managed by proxy; Delane had understood that, and faced it.

Nothing in the whole unprecedented situation was more odd, more unexpected and interesting, than Mr. Gracy's own perception of it. He too had become aware that his case was without alternative.

"They *had* to have me here, by gad; I see that myself. Old firebrand like me ... couldn't be trusted! Hayley saw it from the first—fine fellow, my son-in-law. He made no bones about telling me so. Said: I can't trust you, father' ... said it right out to me. By gad, if he'd talked to me like that a few years sooner I don't answer for the consequences! But I ain't my own man any longer.... I've got to put up with being treated like a baby.... I forgave him on the spot, sir—on the spot." His fine eye filled, and he stretched a soft old hand, netted with veins and freckles, across the table to me.

In the virtual seclusion imposed by his presence I was one of the few friends the Delanes still saw. I knew Leila was grateful to me for coming; but I did not need that incentive. It was enough that I could give even a negative support to Delane. The first months were horrible; but he was evidently saying to himself: "Things will settle down gradually," and just squaring his great shoulders to the storm.

Things didn't settle down; as embodied in Bill Gracy they continued in a state of effervescence. Filial care, good food and early hours restored the culprit to comparative health; he became exuberant, arrogant and sly. Happily his first imprudence caused a relapse alarming even to himself. He saw that his powers of resistance were gone, and, tremulously tender over his own plight, he relapsed into a plaintive burden. But he was never a passive one. Some part or other he had to play, usually to somebody's detriment.

One day a strikingly dressed lady forced her way in to see him, and the house echoed with her recriminations. Leila objected to the children's assisting at such scenes, and when Christmas brought the boys home she sent them to Canada with a tutor, and herself went with the little girl to Florida. Delane, Gracy and I sat down alone to our Christmas turkey, and I wondered what Delane's queer friend of the Washington hospital would have thought of that festivity. Mr. Gracy was in a melting mood, and reviewed his past with an edifying prolixity. "After all, women and children have always loved me," he summed up, a tear on his lashes. "But I've been a curse to you and Leila, and I know it, Hayley. That's my only merit, I suppose—that I *do* know it! Well, here's to turning over a new leaf ..." and so forth.

One day, a few months later, Mr. Broad, the head of the firm, sent for me. I was surprised, and somewhat agitated, at the summons, for I was not often called into his august presence.

"Mr. Delane has a high regard for your ability," he began affably.

I bowed, thrilled at what I supposed to be a hint of promotion; but Mr. Broad went on: "I know you are at his house a great deal. In spite of the difference in age he always speaks of you as an old friend." Hopes of promotion faded, yet left me unregretful. Somehow, this was even better. I bowed again.

Mr. Broad was becoming embarrassed. "You see Mr. William Gracy rather frequently at his son-in-law's?"

"He's living there," I answered bluntly.

Mr. Broad heaved a sigh. "Yes. It's a fine thing of Mr. Delane ... but does he quite realize the consequences? His own family side with his wife. You'll wonder at my speaking with such frankness ... but I've been asked ... it has been suggested...."

"If he weren't there he'd be in the gutter."

Mr. Broad sighed more deeply. "Ah, it's a problem.... You may ask why I don't speak directly to Mr. Delane ... but it's so delicate, and he's so uncommunicative. Still, there are Institutions.... You don't feel there's anything to be done?"

I was silent, and he shook hands, murmured: "This is confidential," and made a motion of dismissal. I withdrew to my desk, feeling that the situation must indeed be grave if Mr. Broad could so emphasize it by consulting me.

New York, to ease its mind of the matter, had finally decided that Hayley Delane was "queer." There were the two of them, madmen both, hobnobbing together under his roof; no wonder poor Leila found the place untenable! That view, bruited about, as such things are, with a mysterious underground rapidity, prepared me for what was to follow.

One day during the Easter holidays I went to dine with the Delanes, and finding my host alone with old Gracy I concluded that Leila had again gone off with the children. She had: she had been gone a week, and had just sent a letter to her husband saying that she was sailing from Montreal with the little girl. The boys would be sent back to Groton with a trusted servant. She would add nothing more, as she did not wish to reflect unkindly on what his own family agreed with her in thinking an act of ill-advised generosity. He knew that she was worn out by the strain he had imposed on her, and would understand her wishing to get away for a while....

She had left him.

Such events were not, in those days, the matters of course they have since become; and I doubt if, on a man like Delane, the blow would ever have fallen lightly. Certainly that evening was the grimmest I ever passed in his company. I had the same impression as on the day of Bolton Byrne's chastisement: the sense that Delane did not care a fig for public opinion. His knowing that it sided with his wife did not, I believe, affect him in the least; nor did her own view of his conduct—and for that I was unprepared. What really ailed him, I discovered, was his loneliness. He missed her, he wanted her back—her trivial irritating presence was the thing in the world he could least dispense with. But when he told me what she had done he simply added: "I see no help for it; we've both of us got a right to our own opinion."

Again I looked at him with astonishment. Another voice seemed to be speaking through his lips, and I had it on mine to say: "Was that what your old friend in Washington would have told you?" But at the door of the dining-room, where we had lingered, Mr. Gracy's flushed countenance and unreverend auburn locks appeared between us.

"Look here, Hayley; what about our little game? If I'm to be packed off to bed at ten like a naughty boy you might at least give me my hand of poker first." He winked faintly at me as we passed into the library, and added, in a hoarse aside: "If he thinks he's going to boss me like Leila he's mistaken. Flesh and blood's one thing; now she's gone I'll be damned if I take any bullying."

That threat was the last flare of Mr. Gracy's indomitable spirit. The act of defiance which confirmed it brought on a severe attack of pleurisy. Delane nursed the old man with dogged patience, and he emerged from the illness diminished, wizened, the last trace of auburn gone from his scant curls, and nothing left of his old self but a harmless dribble of talk.

Delane taught him to play patience, and he used to sit for hours by the library fire, puzzling over the cards, or talking to the children's parrot, which he fed and tended with a touching regularity. He also devoted a good deal of time to collecting stamps for his youngest grandson, and his increasing gentleness and playful humour so endeared him to the servants that a trusted housemaid had to be dismissed for smuggling cocktails into his room. On fine days Delane, coming home earlier from the bank, would take him for a short stroll; and one day, happening to walk up Fifth Avenue behind them, I noticed that the younger man's broad shoulders were beginning to stoop like the other's, and that there was less lightness in his gait than in Bill Gracy's jaunty shamble. They looked like two old men doing their daily mile on the sunny side of the street. Bill Gracy was no longer a danger to the community, and Leila might have come home. But I understood from Delane that she was still abroad with her daughter.

Society soon grows used to any state of things which is imposed upon it without explanation. I had noticed that Delane never explained; his chief strength lay in that negative quality. He was probably hardly aware that people were beginning to say: "Poor old Gracy—after all, he's making a decent end. It was the proper thing for Hayley to do—but his wife ought to come back and share the burden with him." In important matters he was so careless of public opinion that he was not likely to notice its veering. He wanted Leila to come home; he missed her and the little girl more and more; but for him there was no "ought" about the matter.

And one day she came. Absence had rejuvenated her, she had some dazzling new clothes, she had made the acquaintance of a charming Italian nobleman who was coming to New York on the next steamer ... she was ready to forgive her husband, to be tolerant, resigned and even fond. Delane, with his amazing simplicity, took all this for granted; the effect of her return was to make him feel he had somehow been in the wrong, and he was ready to bask in her forgiveness. Luckily for her own popularity she arrived in time to soothe her parent's declining moments. Mr. Gracy was now a mere mild old pensioner and Leila used to drive out with him regularly, and refuse dull invitations "because she had to be with Papa."

After all, people said, she had a heart. Her husband thought so too, and triumphed in the conviction. At that time life under the Delane roof, though melancholy, was idyllic; it was a pity old Gracy could not have been kept alive longer, so miraculously did his presence unite the household it had once divided. But he was beyond being aware of this, and from a cheerful senility sank into coma and death. The funeral was attended by the whole of New York, and Leila's crape veil was of exactly the right length—a matter of great importance in those days.

Life has a way of overgrowing its achievements as well as its ruins. In less time than seemed possible in so slow-moving a society, the Delane's family crisis had been smothered and forgotten. Nothing seemed changed in the mutual attitude of husband and wife, or in that of their little group toward the couple. If anything, Leila had gained in popular esteem by her assiduity at her father's bedside; though as a truthful chronicler I am bound to add that she partly forfeited this advantage by plunging into a flirtation with the Italian nobleman before her crape trimmings had been replaced by *passementerie*. On such fundamental observances old New York still took its stand.

As for Hayley Delane, he emerged older, heavier, more stooping, but otherwise unchanged, from the ordeal. I am not sure that anyone except myself was aware that there had been an ordeal. But my conviction remained. His wife's return had changed him back into a card-playing, ball-going, race-frequenting elderly gentleman; but I had seen the waters part, and a granite rock thrust up from them. Twice the upheaval had taken place; and each time in obedience to motives unintelligible to the people he lived among. Almost any man can take a stand on a principle his fellow-citizens are already occupying; but Hayley Delane held out for things his friends could not comprehend, and did it for reasons he could not explain. The central puzzle subsisted.

Does it subsist for me to this day? Sometimes, walking up town from the bank where in my turn I have become an institution, I glance through the rails of Trinity churchyard and wonder. He has lain there ten years or more now; his wife has married the President of a rising Western University, and grown intellectual and censorious; his children are scattered and established. Does the old Delane vault hold his secret, or did I surprise it one day; did he and I surprise it together?

It was one Sunday afternoon, I remember, not long after Bill Gracy's edifying end. I had not gone out of town that week-end, and after a long walk in the frosty blue twilight of Central Park I let myself into my little flat. To my surprise I saw Hayley Delane's big overcoat and tall hat in the hall.

He used to drop in on me now and then, but mostly on the way home from a dinner where we happened to have met; and I was rather startled at his appearance at that hour and on a Sunday. But he lifted an untroubled face from the morning paper.

"You didn't expect a call on a Sunday? Fact is, I'm out of a job. I wanted to go down to the country, as usual, but there's some grand concert or other that Leila was booked for this afternoon; and a dinner tonight at Alstrop's. So I dropped in to pass the time of day. What *is* there to do on a Sunday afternoon, anyhow?"

There he was, the same old usual Hayley, as much put to it as the merest fribble of his set to employ an hour unfilled by poker! I was glad he viewed me as a possible alternative, and laughingly told him so. He laughed too—we were on terms of brotherly equality—and told me to go ahead and read two or three notes which had arrived in my absence. "Gad—how they shower down on a fellow at your age!" he chuckled.

I broke the seals and was glancing through the letters when I heard an exclamation at my back.

"By Jove—there he is!" Hayley Delane shouted. I turned to see what he meant.

He had taken up a book—an unusual gesture, but it lay at his elbow, and I suppose he had squeezed the newspapers dry. He held the volume out to me without speaking, his forefinger resting on the open page; his swarthy face was in a glow, his hand shook a little. The page to which his finger pointed bore the steel engraving of a man's portrait.

"It's him to the life—I'd know those old clothes of his again anywhere," Delane exulted, jumping up from his seat.

I took the book and stared first at the portrait and then at my friend.

"Your pal in Washington?"

He nodded excitedly. "That chap I've often told you about—yes!" I shall never forget the way his smile flew out and reached the dimple. There seemed a network of them spangling his happy face. His eyes had grown absent, as if gazing down invisible vistas. At length they travelled back to me.

"How on earth did the old boy get his portrait in a book? Has somebody been writing something about him?" His sluggish curiosity awakened, he stretched his hand for the volume. But I held it back.

"Lots of people have written about him; but this book is his own."

"You mean he wrote it?" He smiled incredulously. "Why, the poor chap hadn't any education!"

"Perhaps he had more than you think. Let me keep the book a moment longer, and read you something from it."

He signed an assent, though I could see the apprehension of the printed page already clouding his interest.

"What sort of things did he write?"

"Things for *you*. Now listen."

He settled back into his armchair, composing a painfully attentive countenance, and I sat down and began:

A sight in camp in the day-break grey and dim,
As from my tent I emerge so early, sleepless,
As slow I walk in the cool fresh air, the path near by the hospital tent,
Three forms I see on stretchers lying, brought out there, untended lying,
Over each the blanket spread, ample brownish woollen blanket,
Grey and heavy blanket, folding, covering all.

Curious, I halt, and silent stand;
Then with light fingers I from the face of the nearest, the first, just lift the blanket:
Who are you, elderly man so gaunt and grim, with well-grey'd hair, and flesh all sunken about the eyes?
Who are you, my dear comrade?

Then to the second I step—And who are you, my child and darling?
Who are you, sweet boy, with cheeks yet blooming?

Then to the third—a face nor child, nor old, very calm, as of beautiful yellow-white ivory;
Young man, I think I know you—I think this face of yours is the face of the Christ himself;
Dead and divine, and brother of all, and here again he lies.

I laid the open book on my knee, and stole a glance at Delane. His face was a blank, still composed in the heavy folds of enforced attention. No spark had been struck from him. Evidently the distance was too great between the far-off point at which he and English poetry had parted company, and this new strange form it had put on. I must find something which would bring the matter closely enough home to surmount the unfamiliar medium.

Vigil strange I kept on the field one night,
When you, my son and my comrade, dropt at my side....

The starlit murmur of the verse flowed on, muffled, insistent; my throat filled with it, my eyes grew dim. I said to myself, as my voice sank on the last line: "He's reliving it all now, seeing it again—knowing for the first time that someone else saw it as he did."

Delane stirred uneasily in his seat, and shifted his crossed legs one over the other. One hand absently stroked the fold of his carefully ironed trousers. His face was still a blank. The distance had not yet been bridged between "Gray's Elegy" and this unintelligible harmony. But I was not discouraged. I ought not to have expected any of it to reach him—not just at first—except by way of the closest personal appeal. I turned from the "Lovely and Soothing Death," at which I had re-opened the book, and looked for another page. My listener leaned back resignedly.

Bearing the bandages, water and sponge,
Straight and swift to my wounded I go....

I read on to the end. Then I shut the book and looked up again. Delane sat silent, his great hands clasping the arms of his chair, his head slightly sunk on his breast. His lids were dropped, as I imagined reverentially. My own heart was beating with a religious emotion; I had never felt the oft-read lines as I felt them then.

A little timidly, he spoke at length. "Did *he* write that?"

"Yes; just about the time you were seeing him, probably."

Delane still brooded; his expression grew more and more timid. "What do you ... er ... call it ... exactly?" he ventured.

I was puzzled for a moment; then: "Why, poetry ... rather a free form, of course.... You see, he was an originator of new verse-forms...."

"New verse-forms?" Delane echoed forlornly. He stood up in his heavy way, but did not offer to take the book from me again. I saw in his face the symptoms of approaching departure.

"Well, I'm glad to have seen his picture after all these years," he said; and on the threshold he paused to ask: "What was his name, by the way?"

When I told him he repeated it with a smile of slow relish. "Yes; that's it. Old Walt—that was what all the fellows used to call him. He was a great chap: I'll never forget him.—I rather wish, though," he added, in his mildest tone of reproach, "you hadn't told me that he wrote all that rubbish."

THE END

Milton Keynes UK
Ingram Content Group UK Ltd.
UKHW012315040624
443649UK00007B/654